D1408338

An Imprint of Sterling Publishing
387 Park Avenue South
New York, NY 10016

SANDY CREEK and the distinctive Sandy Creek logo are trademarks of Barnes and Noble, Inc.

© 2013 by Top That! Publishing plc.

This 2013 edition published by Sandy Creek.

All rights reserved. No part of this publication may be reproduced, stored in a retrieval system or transmitted
in any form or by any means (including electronic, mechanical, photocopying, recording, or otherwise)
without prior written permission from the publisher.

Creative Director—Simon Couchman
Editorial Director—Daniel Graham

Written by Rupert Matthews
Illustrated by Marina Le Ray

ISBN 978-1-4351-4895-6

Manufactured in Nansha, China.
Lot #:
10 9 8 7 6 5 4 3 2 1
05/13

Hide-and-Ghost Seek...

Illustrated by Marina Le Ray
Written by Rupert Matthews

Sandy Creek
NEW YORK

Are you ready to play hide-and-ghost-seek?
Mrs. Skelebones is looking for a missing ghost called Spiro.
Can you help her to search for him in the fog that engulfs the
haunted town of Howlingwood?

There are ten ghosts and ghouls in each scene!
Can you spot them all?

Have You
seen this
ghost?

DESCRIPTION:
WEARS SPECTACLES
AND A BOW TIE

Mrs Skelebones

Inside Chillesford Manor, the spooky servants
are dusting and cleaning. Could Spiro
be hiding somewhere in the haunted hallway?

Spiro is often found at the Witches' Brew Café, drinking a bubbling bat-wing milk shake or munching on a crab-claw cookie. But is he hiding here now?

There's a gruesome game of soccer kicking off between
Phantom Park Rangers and Blood Pool Soccer Club. How many ghouls
are going for a goal in this spooky sporting scene? Is our missing
ghost friend lurking in the shadows?

The Dungeon Club is crowded. Everyone is here to see Spiro's favorite rock group, the Spooky Spiders. Surely he must be hiding in here!

It seems a most unlikely place to find Spiro, but we should look around Wormwood Werewolf Racetrack to make sure he's not hiding in the crowd.

Bone Yard Cemetery is where Spiro might be lurking.
As you may already know, ghosts can't resist
a quick stroll around the tombstones.

On stormy seas, beyond the cliffs
at Sharktooth Shore, a ghostly pirate
ship sets sail. Could it be that Spiro has
joined its creepy pirate crew?

We've searched everywhere for Spiro, and school is finished for today! Is he playing hide-and-ghost-seek with the phantoms in the playground?

It's getting very late and there's still no sign of Spiro!
Where has he been? There's a letter on the office desk.
Perhaps it will explain why he's hiding.

Principal's
-Office-

Dear Mrs. Skelebones,
I am sorry I missed school.
I heard that real live humans
were coming to visit us today.
I think I'm scared of real live
humans. They are so strang
I know I was naughty to
hide, but I didn't know
what else to do.
From,
Spiro

Oh Spiro, you're not naughty, and it's silly to be scared. Humans really aren't that bad when you meet them. Look at that one reading this book and I think you'll agree with me. So next time you feel uncertain and want to hide, talk to someone who cares about you and things won't seem quite so bad!

Did you find Spiro and 100 of his ghostly friends?
If not, the red ghost images highlighted on
each page will help you to spot them all.

There are ten ghosts hiding in each scene.
Turn back to the story to find the ones
you've missed!

Are you ready to play hide-and-ghost-seek?
Mrs. Skelebones is looking for a missing ghost called Spiro.
Can you help her to search for him in the fog that engulfs the
haunted town of Howlingwood?

There are ten ghosts and ghouls in each scene!
Can you spot them all?

There's a gruesome game of soccer kicking off between
Phantom Park Rangers and Blood Pool Soccer Club. How many ghouls
are going for a goal in this spooky sporting scene? Is our missing
ghost friend lurking in the shadows?

The Dungeon Club is crowded. Everyone is here
to see Spiro's favorite rock group, the Spooky
Spiders. Surely he must be hiding in here!

On stormy seas, beyond the cliffs
at Sharktooth Shore, a ghostly pirate
ship sets sail. Could it be that Spiro has
joined its creepy pirate crew?

We've searched everywhere for Spiro, and school is
finished for today! Is he playing hide-and-ghost-seek
with the phantoms in the playground?

Inside Chillesford Manor, the spooky servants are dusting and cleaning. Could Spiro be hiding somewhere in the haunted hallway?

Spiro is often found at the Witches' Brew Café, drinking a bubbling bat-wing milk shake or munching on a crab-claw cookie. But is he hiding here now?

It seems a most unlikely place to find Spiro, but we should look around Wormwood Werewolf Racetrack to make sure he's not hiding in the crowd.

Bone Yard Cemetery is where Spiro might be lurking. As you may already know, ghosts can't resist a quick stroll around the tombstones.

It's getting very late and there's still no sign of Spiro! Where has he been? There's a letter on the office desk. Perhaps it will explain why he's hiding.

Dear Mrs. Skelebones,
I am sorry I missed school. I heard that real live humans were coming to visit us today. I think I'm scared of real live humans. They are so strange! I know I was naughty to hide, but I didn't know what else to do.
From,
Spiro

Oh Spiro, you're not naughty, and it's silly to be scared. Humans really aren't that bad when you meet them. Look at that one reading this book and I think you'll agree with me. So next time you feel uncertain and want to hide, talk to someone who cares about you and things won't seem quite so bad!